Penguins

Liz Pichon

GULLANE
CHILDREN'S BOOKS

It's morning at the zoo.
The penguins wake up and have their first swim.
Penguins tend to do the same thing every day.

Here is a list of...
What Penguins Like To Do The Most.

1. Swim

2. Eat fish
(Fast - before the seagulls pinch them)

3. Play penguin games

4. Sleep standing up

5. Look at the people outside

6. Look at the people through the glass

Most days, nothing very exciting happens.

But today, it's a completely different story . . .

Little Penguin sees
something on the rock.

"DON'T TOUCH IT!"
says Big Penguin. "It belongs
to a person and they'll come
back to find it."

But nobody comes back.
So the penguins move closer for a better look.

"Is it food?" asks Hungry Penguin.
"I don't think so," says Big Penguin.
"It's a camera," Little Penguin squeaks.
"What do you do with a camera?" they ask.
"You smile at it!" grins Little Penguin.

"Are you sure you can't eat it?" asks Hungry Penguin.

"Let's press ALL the buttons!" says Bouncy Penguin, jumping on the camera.

FLASH!

It goes off.

"I DON'T LIKE IT!" cries Big Penguin. "Chill out!" says Little Penguin.

They peer through the camera lens.
"It's **too freaky**," says Big Penguin.

Little Penguin takes the camera.
"Hey everyone, look at me and say FISH!"

"FISH!"

Little Penguin takes a picture.

CLICK!

Now all the penguins want to use the camera.

CLICK!

They take lots and lots of fabulous pictures.

flash!

But suddenly...

. . . the camera stops working!

"Oh dear," says Big Penguin, "we'd better put it back."

So Little Penguin puts the camera back on the rock where he found it.

In the morning, the keeper finds the camera. "I'd better get this to *Lost Property* before those hungry penguins get their beaks on it!"

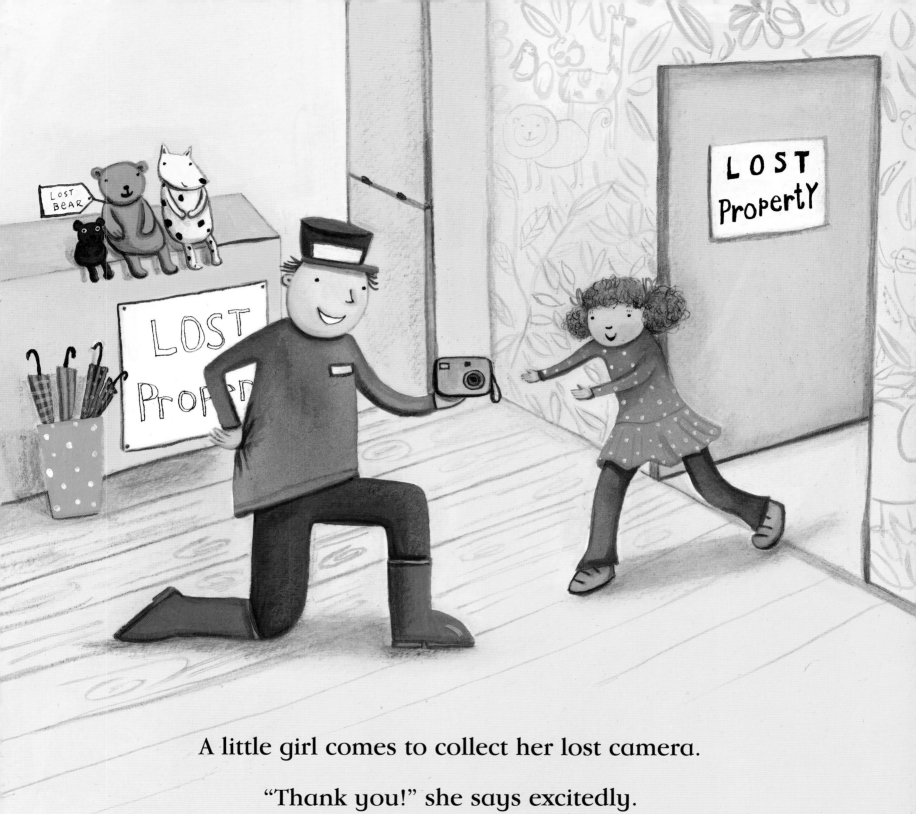

A little girl comes to collect her lost camera.

"Thank you!" she says excitedly.
"I can't wait to see all the
pictures I took at the zoo!"

There are pictures of monkeys, lions, tigers and elephants. And, strangely, there are quite a few pictures of penguins too!